Back at our house, [...]
our special Christmas Eve dinner.

"Set one more place for our surprise guest!" shouted my father, trying to be cheery.

Okay, I thought. This doesn't have to be so bad. After all it *is* still Christmas. So what if Ninnie Poo was at my house? How mean could she be on Christmas Eve?

"These raw oysters vinaigrette are overcooked!" said Nanette, pushing her plate away.

"Why, those are my famous alligator meatballs," said Grandma Lou. "They go perfectly with the southern fried turkey and my cajun vegetable puffs."

"*Merci*, but I am afraid I have lost my appetite," said Nanette. But her face did not look the way her face usually looks when she is trying to be French as usual. Her face looked sad.

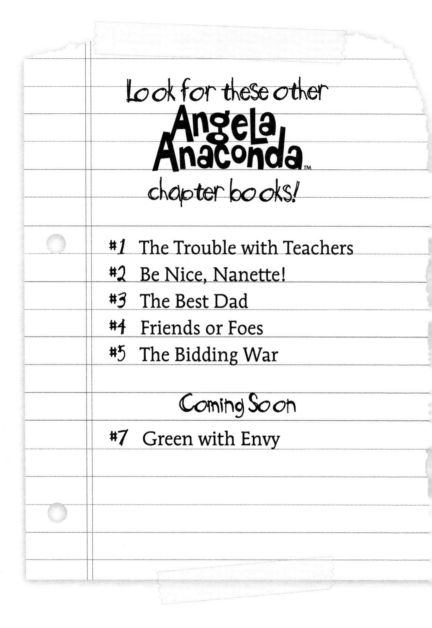

Look for these other
Angela Anaconda™
chapter books!

THE FRIGHT BEFORE CHRISTMAS

If you purchased this book without a cover you should be
aware that this book is stolen property. It was reported as
"unsold and destroyed" to the publisher and neither the author
nor the publisher has received any payment for
this "stripped book."

Based on the TV series *Angela Anaconda*®
created by Joanna Ferrone and Sue Rose as seen on the Fox Family Channel®

SIMON SPOTLIGHT
An imprint of Simon & Schuster Children's Publishing Division
1230 Avenue of the Americas, New York, New York 10020

© 2001 DECODE Entertainment, Inc.
Copyright in Angela Anaconda and all related characters is owned by DECODE
Entertainment Inc. ANGELA ANACONDA is a registered trademark of Honest Art, Inc.
FOX FAMILY and the FAMILY CHANNEL name and logos are the respective trademarks of
Fox and International Family Entertainment.
All rights reserved.

All rights reserved including the right of reproduction in whole or in part in any form.

SIMON SPOTLIGHT and colophon are registered trademarks of Simon & Schuster.

Manufactured in the United States of America

First Edition
2 4 6 8 10 9 7 5 3 1

ISBN 0-689-84055-1

Library of Congress Control Number 00-111609

(family)

Angela Anaconda

THE FRIGHT BEFORE CHRISTMAS

by Barbara Calamari and Joanna Ferrone

illustrated by Elizabeth Brandt

Simon Spotlight

New York   London   Toronto   Sydney   Singapore

CHAPTER ONE

"'Twas the night before Christmas,

When all through the house,

Not a creature was stirring,

Not even a mouse . . ."

Hi, it's me, Angela Anaconda, and I am sitting on our couch with my baby sister, Lulu, reading this famous Christmas poem to her. Usually I would not be trying to read to Lulu because for one thing, she never pays attention, and for another thing, she always tries to eat the pages. But it is Christmastime and I'm trying to be nice. Who cares if Lulu and I don't know what *'twas* means? This is a famous poem with some very famous pictures and it makes me feel like my favorite holiday, Christmas, is almost here.

Some people, like my best friend, Gina Lash, love Thanksgiving best on account of all the food. My other friend Johnny Abatti, who happens to be a boy, likes the Fourth of July because he can spit watermelon pits and set off firecrackers with his Uncle Nicky. Easter is Gordy Rhinehart's favorite. Even though he is allergic to grass, he likes hunting for colored eggs, which he always hand-colors himself. But for me, Angela Anaconda, Christmas is the very best and most perfect holiday of the year. That is until something very not so perfect happened last year that I'm about to tell you about.

Last Christmas I was sure I was going to have the best Christmas ever. When we made our annual, every-year, family Christmas card, I didn't even mind that I was the only one who looked horrible in the picture. My mom said it was so hard to get Baby Lulu to look at the camera that when she finally did, it was just too bad for me that my eyes weren't all the way open. My two dork-faced brothers said that I looked really good for a gerbil and then they knocked their big block heads together because they thought they were so funny. Anyway, this was the one picture where Baby Lulu was finally looking at the camera and even smiling, so that was the card we sent out to everyone we know, and even a bunch of people we didn't know.

Merry Christmas *from the* Anacond

"Okay," I said to myself. "Better luck next time, Angela Anaconda. But from here on in this is going to be a great Christmas! Maybe even the best Christmas ever!"

First of all, that year I picked out a really good present, not like some years when you can't decide and you end up getting things like underwear and books. That year I knew exactly what I wanted—a pair of real, authentic, arctic snowshoes just like the explorers wore for walking on top of the snow. While everyone else was getting snow in the tops of their boots and having to go inside with wet socks and frostbite, I, Angela Anaconda, would be outside having fun with my warm, dry feet. Plus, I'd be taller by as many actual inches as it actually snowed. All I knew was that I really wanted those snowshoes!

I also knew the best way to get other people

to get you something YOU really want is to get them things THEY really want, even if they don't know they really want it until you give it to them. And even though my two brothers, Derek and Mark (who if you ask me, both look like gerbils all the time), are Neanderthals, when I saw these supersonic slingshots that fire real rocks hundreds of feet in the air, I knew that they both had to have them, so I bought them those. My Mom calls this the Christmas spirit. I call it the once-a-year-when-you-give-nice-things-even-to-idiots-so-they'll-give-you-nice-things-back spirit. Whatever you call it, I was sure it was going to be the best Christmas ever.

CHAPTER TWO

Two days after I went and bought Derek and Mark their presents, I put my secret plan into action. I left the supersonic slingshot boxes sitting on my bed.

Now I'm used to Derek and Mark always torturing me. Usually they call me stupid things like "Angiepants" and make fun of everything I say or do. So you'd probably guess that I was very surprised when I happened to hear them saying nice things about me. Okay, so what I wanted to know was if they did not know I was secretly overhearing them, by accident on account of my ear was pressed against their door, did it actually count that they were saying nice things?

"Gosh, Angiepants got us good gifts for a change," said Mark.

"We can fire real rocks and everything," said Derek.

"The only bummer is now we have to get her something good too," said Mark.

"Bummer, dude," said Derek.

"Yes!" I whispered to myself as I snuck back to my own room and saw that the slingshot boxes were opened and all the tissue paper was messed up. Not only did Mark and Derek know that I got them great gifts for Christmas, but now they would have to get me something great too. My plan was working.

So later that day, my two brothers asked

me what I wanted for Christmas. This was easier than I thought.

"Snowshoes," I told them. "That's the most important thing on my list."

Instead of saying something insulting to me about my choice of gift and how I would never get it, all they said was, "Snowshoes. All right, you got it, Angela!"

Like most older brothers who are grunting cavemen, my brothers play football on the high school team. Now Coach Rhinehart, who is my friend Gordy Rhinehart's father, has a Christmas party for the football team every year. Gordy makes his famous chocolate soufflé, and Coach Rhinehart makes his famous eggnog, and all those weird grunting Stone Age football players stand around and sing Christmas carols. So last year at the party Mark and Derek had a discussion with Gordy, which I did not know about until later when it was too late. But, never mind, this is what they said:

"What are you going to get Angela for Christmas?" Gordy asked my brothers.

"We have to get her something good this year," said Mark.

"Yeah, she wants snowshoes," said Derek.

"Snowshoes?" asked Gordy. He was very surprised to hear this. "I didn't realize Angela Anaconda liked those sorts of things."

Now Gordy Rhinehart is one of my best friends, but he and I are very different when it comes to stuff we like to play with.

"Well, that's what she wants!" said Derek. "Do you know where we can get some?"

Gordy pulled out his favorite *Catalogue of Classic Toys.* "Here she is, doll number thirteen in the Country Girl Doll Collection: 'Snowshoes'!" said Gordy. "These dolls are

expensive, but they're of the highest quality. Snowshoes is a lovely little Arctic princess dressed in genuine white fur with white patent leather après-ski snowshoes!"

"Angela wants one of those?" said Mark.

"I've never seen her with a doll before!" said Derek.

"Maybe that's because no one's ever thought to buy her one before," replied Gordy, trying to be helpful. "Every girl should have at least one Country Girl Doll; they're collectibles!"

"Maybe you're right, she does have a bug collection," said Mark.

"Dude, look at how much money this doll costs!" said Derek.

"That's like mowing the lawn twenty times," said Mark.

"Yeah, but she did get us those slingshots. So if this is what she really wants, we have to get it," said Derek.

CHAPTER THREE

Now if anyone knows me at all, they know I do not like dressed-up dolls that sit in a case that you cannot do anything with. And that is probably why Nanette Manoir owns every one of those dolls and thinks every girl on Earth wants useless boring things that are not toys and are not fun. And as you probably know by now, Ninnie Wart Manoir is my biggest enemy on Earth and in the universe, and nothing, not even

Christmas or the Christmas spirit, could get her to be nice to anyone.

You would almost think Nanette's snooty parents know this about her because they went away to get a suntan before all of their Christmas activities, and they left their precious pet with Alfredo, their butler. And I know this on account of when Johnny Abatti and I were out throwing snowballs in a sneak attack on their house, we saw the Manoirs saying good-bye to their little fake French spoiled brat.

"If you're going away and leaving me here, then I want something *très* special for Christmas this year," said Nanette.

"And Mumsy and I aim to get it for you," said her father.

"We'll be home two days before Christmas," Nanette's mom promised, "with all kinds of wonderful gifts for our precious angel."

"And you better come back *tout de suite!*" said Nanette, stomping her foot and pretending to be French. "I do *not* want to be stuck with Alfredo any longer than necessary!" Alfredo did not look very happy to be stuck with Ninnie Poo either. And Johnny and I were not so happy either, because when Nasty Nin saw us standing there she screamed at us for trespassing and ordered Alfredo to chase us away.

CHAPTER FOUR

Two days later it was Christmas Eve (the night before Christmas) and I was still thinking it was going to be the best Christmas ever. For starters, my brothers couldn't wait to get their hands on those slingshots.

"How about we open the presents we bought for one another right now?" asked Mark.

"Yeah, we want to see Miss Angiepants's

face when she opens our gift," said Derek, talking about me like I wasn't even there, as usual.

"You're going to owe us big time!" said Mark.

Could it be that my brothers actually bought me what I wanted for Christmas? I thought to myself.

"Can we open our presents now, Mom?" I begged. "It *is* Christmas Eve."

"There's more to Christmas than just getting presents," she said. "Besides, you know we don't open gifts until after we eat Grandma Lou's special Christmas dinner!"

Now Grandma Lou is from Florida, and she is one of my most favorite people on Earth. And her Christmas dinners *are* very special. But because she is a grandma, she does *not* do things at kid speed, which means she takes her time and only does things when she is ready to do them, and that includes cooking Christmas dinner.

I went into the kitchen to see if I could help make her go faster. But, instead of cooking, she was looking out the window at the falling snow.

"Its been years since I've seen a white Christmas," she exclaimed. "It reminds me of when I was a girl. We'd all bundle up and go out caroling. I sure do miss it."

"Some of the neighbors still go every year. Let's join in!" exclaimed my father.

"Sounds like a plan to me!" yelled Grandma Lou. "My special Christmas dinner can wait."

Oh, brother . . . I couldn't believe my ears. Dinner wasn't even started and now we had to go Christmas caroling! I was getting worried I was never going to open my present!

Now, I didn't know it at the time, but over at her house, Nanette was starting to get worried too. You see, Mr. and Mrs. Manoir, her parents, were still not home from their tanning trip. And that could only mean two things for her: no presents, and she was stuck with Alfredo. Anyway, what no one knew then, is that Nanette's parents were the ones who were really stuck on account of they skidded off the road and drove their car into a snowbank because of all the snow. So there was Alfredo with his worst nightmare coming true, which was to be stuck with Nanette Manoir on Christmas Eve; and there was Nanette without her parents, which meant she was not going to get the super-special Christmas gifts she wanted.

CHAPTER FIVE

Now, I don't know about you, but going around in the freezing cold, Christmas caroling with your friends and old people does not seem all that fun to me. Having to wait even longer to open your best Christmas gift ever, and singing for people like Mr. and Mrs. Brinks (she is my teacher) at their front door on one of your most favorite nights of the year, is more like my idea of a Christmas nightmare. But that is what me and my family were doing. And we were not alone.

There were more people Christmas caroling than were home in their houses. Johnny Abatti came with his Uncle Nicky and they even got Nonna out of the pizza parlor for the night. Josephine Praline handed out sheets with the words to holy songs. Gordy Rhinehart and his dad, Coach Rhinehart, even brought along Gina Lash and her mom, who do not even celebrate Christmas. (They'll probably make us do some Chanukah thing, which we won't want to do, for Chanukah next year.) And everyone, except me, seemed to be having a great time. I just wanted to get home, out of this freezing cold, and open our Christmas presents, which by the way, if we had already opened I'd be wearing my snowshoes and wouldn't mind being out in the snow at all.

How many Christmas songs do Mr. and Mrs. Brinks need to hear? I wondered.

The only good thing about caroling that night was that Gordy Rhinehart told me that I would love my present from Derek and Mark.

"I'm not going to say another word, Angela Anaconda, but I *will* give you the first letter. It starts with an 'S.'"

"Well," I said to Gordy, secretly knowing he meant snowshoes, "as you know, it's not the gift, but the thought that counts, especially if the thought starts with 'S.'"

Then before I could ask him if it really was a pair of snowshoes, Josephine Praline made an announcement: "The next house we will be performing at contains a sad little girl whose parents are lost in the snow. Let's do the best we can to cheer her up!"

I must admit, I *did* wonder who this sad

little girl could be. And I *did* feel sorry for her. After all, here I was with my entire family and my very best friends, singing songs on my most favorite holiday, just waiting to go home and get the present I had most wanted to get. Because, as I told you earlier, I had a feeling that this was going to be the best Christmas ever.

CHAPTER SIX

"Does anyone know who the sad little girl *is?*" asked Gordy Rhinehart. And even Gina Lash, the smartest girl in our class, did not know.

"We should be sending her a pizza," said Nonna. "But here we are, instead, singing her songs! What's a matter with this country?"

Uncle Nicky kept wiping his eyes because stories about sad little girls seem to be even sadder at Christmastime.

As we came around the corner heading

right for Nanette's giant pink house, I turned to my friend Johnny. "We can't be going to where I think we're going. Josephine Praline said 'sad little girl', not 'nasty little Nanette.'"

But we *were* going to where I thought we were going. Just as we all started to sing our most gentle Christmas song, the front door of the Manoir house flew open.

"Alfredo, come quickly! There are a bunch of uninvited guests screeching on our front steps, trespassing on our private property!"

Can you believe it? The sad little girl was none other than Nanette Manoir!

"How can you be so cruel?" she screamed. "You come here singing Christmas carols when my poor parents are lost in the snow along with my many expensive gifts!"

"Poor, Nanette, alone at Christmas," said Josephine.

Poor Alfredo! I thought. Here he was, stuck with this screaming girl, when all he wanted was to go home to his own house for Christmas, which was exactly what I was feeling myself!

I was just starting to think things couldn't get much worse, when suddenly they did.

"Just because my parents haven't come back," shrieked Nanette, "doesn't mean I asked for any of *you* to come here!"

"Oh, you poor child, you must be crazy with grief," I heard my mother say. "Wouldn't you like to come home and have some Christmas dinner with us?"

What did she say?

"Come on, young 'un, I can easily set another place at the Christmas table," said Grandma Lou.

"What wonderful people you are!" said Alfredo. "A sweet, kind family, just what

Mademoiselle Nanette desperately needs!" And before anyone could say anything about it, Alfredo pushed Nanette out the door, threw her her hat and coat, and ran off to be with his family. At least *he* got to be happy on Christmas Eve.

Nanette turned to me. "Christmas at *your* house, Angela Anaconda? Alfredo, come back here or my missing parents will fire you!" Then she started to sniffle and said, "That is, if they're ever found."

When Nanette began to cry, even my dork-brained brothers felt sorry for her.

"Gee, we should try to do something nice for Nanette," said Mark.

"None of us have ever been without our family at Christmas," said Derek.

"I want Christmas the way I want it!" screamed Nanette as my mom and dad led her down the driveway.

"Those Anacondas are nice people," Nonna said to Uncle Nicky who was still wiping his eyes.

"This is a beautiful Christmas story," said Josephine Praline.

Beautiful for everyone else, I felt like telling them.

Only Gina Lash knew what kind of night we were going to have with Grinchy Poo Manoir around.

"Good luck, Angela Anaconda," she said to me. "And try to have a Merry Christmas."

CHAPTER SEVEN

Back at our house, 'twas almost time for our special Christmas Eve dinner.

"Set one more place for our surprise guest!" shouted my father, trying to be cheery.

Okay, I thought. This doesn't have to be so bad. After all it *is* still Christmas. So what if Ninnie Poo was at my house? How mean could she be on Christmas Eve?

"These raw oysters vinaigrette are over-cooked!" said Nanette, pushing her plate away.

"Why, those are my famous alligator meatballs," said Grandma Lou. "They go perfectly with the southern fried turkey and my cajun vegetable puffs."

"Last Christmas we had a catered meal from Chef Louis, the only four star restaurant in the state," said Nanette. "I'm afraid this doesn't compare."

"We have some leftover vegetable fried rice that was catered from the Tapwater Springs Chinese restaurant," said my dad, trying to be nice once again.

"*Merci*, but I am afraid I have lost my appetite," said Nanette. But her face did not look the way her face usually looks when she is trying to be French as usual. Her face looked sad.

Maybe, just maybe, I thought, she really does miss her parents.

"After dinner," said my mom, "we'll

finish decorating our tree. Maybe you'd like to help us, Nanette?"

"At my house, that's a job we leave for the hired help. I don't know the first thing about decorating trees, and I'm afraid my sensitive skin might get scratched by those scraggly branches," said Nanette, making believe she was better than everyone else and trying to pretend she wasn't at all sad.

There was nothing we could do to make Nanette happy. And we knew this on account of we all tried. Well, all except me, of course, because I already knew you couldn't make Nanette happy. Besides, I needed to go do a little Christmas investigating in Derek and Mark's room. I could not wait one minute longer to have a look at my best Christmas present ever, and after sitting through dinner with our surprise nightmare guest, I thought I deserved at least a peek.

CHAPTER EIGHT

Everyone, including my dim-bulb brothers, was too busy waiting on unhappy little Ninnie Winnie to notice me leaving the table.

As I creeped into my brothers' room I could hear my whole family trying to make Nanette feel better. Something told me that what I was looking for would definitely not be gift wrapped and tied with a bow. Grunting cavemen do not wrap gifts.

"Aha! There's a bag with something smashed into it," I whispered to myself. The bag looked kind of small. Maybe they got me the wrong size snowshoes, I thought. And it would figure that they would get the size mixed up. But I was wrong about that because when I looked in the bag I realized that my brothers did not get me the gift I wanted for Christmas at all. What they got me was not the *best* present, but the *worst* present!

"A doll! A stupid, useless doll!" I could not believe it. This sure was turning out to be one horrible Christmas. First, I am nice to everyone (which isn't easy) and I buy everyone great gifts. Second, I am made to believe that my brothers are going to buy me the gift I want most in the world. (Remind me to have a word with Gordy Rhinehart.) Third, I have to wait to open the gift I want

most in the world because we have to go out Christmas caroling. Fourth, we get to bring home the nightmare that is Nanette Manoir and have her in our house (enough said). And fifth, and worst of all, the gift I want most in the world ends up being a stupid, useless doll that my even stupider and more useless brothers have bought me and NOT a pair of snowshoes like I wanted!

As I was getting madder and madder (and right before I was about to get as mad as I could ever get,) I heard my mom calling me. "Angela, come down quickly. Nanette is reciting a Christmas poem in French."

"That does it," I said to myself. "Now a Christmas that was already ruined is about to be ruined even more." Then I noticed something I had not noticed before, the name of this useless doll on the bottom of the box: Snowshoes. Could it be that Mark and Derek really thought this was what I meant when I asked them for snowshoes? Could it be that they really were trying to be nice for a change and they just made an honest mistake, which any two nitwits, or even halfway smart brothers, could easily have made?

Now what was I going to do?

"Hey, Angiepants!" It was Mark calling from the living room. "It's time to open our presents! Come on down!"

CHAPTER NINE

Time to open presents? The moment we had all been waiting for and now I just wished it would go away. I had to sneak out of my brothers' room and go get my gifts that I had gotten for everyone else. I was so busy thinking about how to pretend I didn't hate the terrible gift my brothers were about to give me, that it made me totally forget about the terrible Christmas guest who was now sitting in our living room.

"A little hot cocoa, Nanette?" asked my mother.

"Not unless it is pure Belgian *chocolat*," said Nanincompoop.

Bah! Humbug! My most favorite holiday, totally ruined. Then, it did not get any better as I watched my brothers jump for joy over those cool, supersonic slingshots I bought them.

"Hey, let's shoot some of those Christmas ornaments into the next yard!"

"Later, dude, its time for Angiepants to open her present and be grateful to us for the rest of our lives."

"Let's see what Grandma Lou got first!" I said. They looked at me like I was crazy. It is a known fact in our house that all anyone ever gives Grandma is soap and other boring stuff you might give your teacher as a gift at the end of the year.

Grandma Lou didn't even bother to unwrap her present. She just sniffed it and said, "Mmmm, sandalwood, my favorite, you shouldn't have."

Between watching everyone else open their presents and Nanette crying over missing her parents, I wanted to scream. And one thing was for sure, the big moment was about to happen. It was now my turn to open the present from Derek and Mark.

"She is not going to believe this!" said Derek as Mark carried the shopping bag in.

"The boys worked very hard to get this for you, Angela," said my mother.

"We're very proud of you fellows," said my dad.

Oh, great, I thought to myself. Not only have they bought me the worst possible gift, but now they are getting special attention and compliments for it too.

"Ta-da!" said Mark as he dropped the bag into my lap.

Then Derek said, "Open it!" because I was taking too long.

"I just want to savor this beautiful wrapping," I said. They all stared at me. Even Nanette stopped crying long enough to watch me pull the present out of the bag. I gulped, not knowing how to react, then took a deep breath and put my hand in.

"SNOWSHOES!" a very happy voice screeched, but it was not mine. "Oh, Angela Anaconda, you are the luckiest girl on Earth, or even France! What I would give for a Snowshoes doll!" It was Nanette who was doing the screaming. And for the first time that night, she looked happy, so happy she was jumping up and down. She batted her eyes at Mark and then at Derek and said, "You two must be the greatest brothers a girl

51

could ever have if she had them!"

And that was when I got my idea. "You actually like this doll, Nanette?" I asked.

"Is there anyone in the world who doesn't?" she asked.

"Then Merry Christmas, Nanette Manoir," I said with a big smile on my face. "She's all yours!"

CHAPTER TEN

"Are you serious? Oh, Angela Anaconda, I will cherish it all of my life," sobbed Nanette, and because it would be totally gross if she had kissed *me*, she reached over and kissed Baby Lulu on the head.

"Child," said Grandma Lou very softly to me, "that is the true meaning of Christmas."

You mean giving away a stupid doll that I never wanted? I wanted to say.

But the truth is, giving that Snowshoes

doll (which I never wanted) to someone who really did want it (I don't know why), *did* make me feel good.

My mom had tears in her eyes. "I am so proud of you," she said. Even Derek and Mark were happy because Nanette kept saying that it was the best gift anyone could ever get. My dad patted me on the head and was about to put on more Christmas music when our doorbell rang.

"Who could it be at this hour?" asked my mom.

"It better not be any more Christmas carolers," said Derek.

"If it is, we can shoot them with our slingshots," said Mark.

My dad opened the door and there stood Mr. and Mrs. Manoir, looking like two snowmen.

"We're looking for our precious angel,"

Mr. Manoir said weakly. He was covered in snow.

"Mummy! Daddy!" Nanette ran and kissed them both.

"Our car broke down and we walked the entire way back from the tanning spa to be with our little angel for Christmas," said Mrs. Manoir, leaning against the door. "Ouch! My feet are killing me!"

"Come on in and warm up!" said my mom.

"Oh, I don't want to track snow on your carpet even if it is synthetic. Someone please help me out of these ridiculous contraptions!" Mrs. Manoir said. "I never want to see these again!" she added as she pointed down at something big and shiny and super-deluxe on her feet. And you know what she was pointing at? A pair of snowshoes.

"You mean it?" I asked.

"Yes, of course. Be a nice little girl and get rid of them for me."

"No problem!" I exclaimed as I carefully took Mrs. Manoir's snowshoes off her feet.

Then Nanette showed her parents her Snowshoes doll. "I know it's hard to believe, given that we're in this little hovel, but this has turned out to be a very good Christmas!" she exclaimed.

Now, I know I never agree with Nanette Manoir on anything (I mean anything!), but this time I had to agree with her. And you know what? So did everyone else.

"Can I get anyone some hot cocoa?" asked my mom.

"Is it pure Belgian *chocolat?*" asked Mrs. Manoir.

Like I said, last year I was sure I was going to have the best Christmas ever. And after the Manoirs finally left, it only got merrier. Then everybody kissed good night, even my brothers, which was nice but also really gross, and we went to bed.

But I was so happy and excited about my new snowshoes that I couldn't go to sleep. And as I watched the snow fall outside the window, I realized that this really had been a special night. Even though Derek and Mark are a couple of blockheads, they were only trying to be nice. I opened up that Christmas book again, the one I had been reading to Lulu, and instead of seeing the famous picture, I thought I saw me, Angela Anaconda, dressed in a nightgown and nightcap, and peering out the window on a starry night before Christmas. . . .

WAS THE NIGHT BEFORE CHRISTM..
WHEN ALL THROUGH MY HOUSE,
NOT A CREATURE WAS STIRRING
ON ACCOUNT OF WE WENT OUT
TO SING WITH OUR NEIGHBORS
SOME SONGS OF GOOD CHEER.
WHEN WHAT TO MY WONDERING
EYES SHOULD APPEAR,
BUT NANETTE AND ALFREDO
AND NIN WAS IN TEARS.
"COME OVER TO OUR HOUSE,"
MY MOM AND DAD ASKED HER.
"TRY GRANDMA LOU'S COOKIN',
SHE ALWAYS MAKES EXTRA,"
"OH, BROTHER," I WHISPERED,
"IT CANNOT BE TRUE,
THIS NIGHT IS NOW RUINED
BY NINCOM-P.U."
AND JUST WHEN I THOUGHT
THAT THINGS COULDN'T BE MORE
REGRETTABLE
I FOUND OUT MY BROTHERS
HAD BOUGHT ME A COLLECTIBLE.
AND EVEN THOUGH I HATED IT,
I HAD TO MAKE THEM THINK

THAT I ACTUALLY LIKED IT,
AND DIDN'T THINK IT STINKED.
THEN I GOT AN IDEA LIKE A BANG ON THE HEAD,
SINCE NIN LOVED THIS DOLL
SHE COULD HAVE IT INSTEAD.
THIS MADE ME FEEL EXCELLENT
DON'T ASK ME WHY—
A FEELING MY DAD WOULD CALL
"MONEY CAN'T BUY."

BUT WHEN BUNNY AND HOWELL,
NINNIE'S PARENTS, GOT HERE
WE WEREN'T TOO SORRY TO SAY,
"SEE YOU NEXT YEAR!"

TWAS THE NIGHT BEFORE
CHRISTMAS,
WHAT I ASKED FOR, I GOT;
I GOT MORE THAN I ASKED FOR,
BELIEVE IT OR NOT!

ABOUT THE AUTHORS

Barbara Calamari and Joanna Ferrone are a team of writers who live and work in New York City. Barbara has written a lot of Angela Anaconda books and Joanna is the show creator who first thought Angela up. You might ask yourself how does this qualify them to write an Angela Anaconda Christmas story? Well, it doesn't, but both of them have experienced more Christmases than they care to mention and both of them hope you like this story. And if you don't, they can always blame each other.

Hi, it's me again, ANGELA ANACONDA, and I JUST WANTED TO SAY IF YOU LIKED THAT STORY THAT YOU JUST READ (OR EVEN IF YOU DIDN'T) YOU'LL REALLY LIKE THIS STORY. IT'S CALLED The Bidding War, AND IT'S CHAPTER BOOK #5. HERE'S AN EXCERPT FROM IT:

THE BIDDING WAR

I was so excited that I couldn't even believe it. Astronaut Bob's space helmet was mine at last! I ran up onto the stage and grabbed it from Spangly Jangles, and put it right on my head.

And just like that, I imagined that I was floating in space with Astronaut Bob the astronaut, and wearing my new space helmet, and drinking special astronaut smoothies through a special astronaut straw that lets you drink while wearing a helmet. And just as I was starting to really enjoy myself, I thought I heard Astronaut Bob say, "*Excusez-moi*, but that will be . . . fifteen dollars."

What fifteen dollars? I thought to myself.

Then someone pulled the helmet off my head. And to my surprise, it wasn't Astronaut Bob talking, but Ninny-Wart Manoir herself.

"I'm bidding fifteen dollars for Astronaut Bob's astronaut helmet," said the Queen of Mean Manoir.

"B-but . . . ," I stammered. "Fourteen dollars and twenty-three cents is all I have!"

"Well then," said Spangly, "looks like the helmet doesn't go to this future astronaut. Looks like the helmet goes to the little French girl who has more money." And with that he banged his gavel. "Sold!"

Nanette held the helmet in her hands. "This will make a *très bien* bowl for my imported French goldfish," she said with a smirk that looked like the knot you tie in the bottom of a balloon. . . .